I0652929

Misjudgment on land
forgetful of its motion
-- not so on the sea

Johnny Flaherty

Perfectly Round Ripples

(made by a jagged stone)

J. Flaherty

Other Books by J.Flaherty:

Ebbing and Fibbing

Gimme Liberty I Can Smell !

Perfectly Round Ripples

© 2020 by J.Flaherty. All rights reserved.
Book design: Johnny Flaherty
Technical furtherance: Kelley Flaherty
Front cover photo: Johnny Flaherty
Back cover photo: Don Tassone
Illustration of author: Dan Olivere
e-mail: neobeatpoet@aol.com

www.Amazon.com
First Edition

ISBN-13: 978-0-578-67226-7

Acknowledgements:

I would like to thank the Pond for its subtle epiphany.
And also the Sea for its stark reality.
And the Cosmos for providing hints of truth.

Contents:

1. Turning Falling Into Fluttering

2. Jagged Stories

3. The Scales of Fortuity

Some rhyme, some refuse
some are truer than others
-- like a porkpie hat

1. Turning Falling Into Fluttering

Perfectly Round Ripples

I tossed a golf ball into the pond
where it made perfectly round ripples
that travelled all the way
to the farthest shores

then I tossed a jagged stone into the pond
and it, too, made perfectly round ripples
that travelled all the way
to the farthest shores

next, I found an old sneaker
with laces missing
and tossed it into the pond
which brought on a thumping splash
causing geese and turtles to turn
their heads, but soon lose interest
as it made perfectly round ripples
that travelled all the way
to the farthest shores

now, should the deeds we perpetrate
here on earth, good or evil,
planned or accidental,
make perfectly round ripples
that travel all the way
to the farthest shores
of the *cosmic* sea,
so mote it be

we shall, for sure, receive our due
somewhere
in the unflinching residuum

Proffered Hands

Drink a tall glass of whiskey
after the wake is over
then forego another 'til
the moon returns to new
hum a few bars of memories
spinning a bluesy eulogy
a soulful sinner in a surreal pulpit
congregation nodding through their tears

Do not run from the grief monster
stand your ground and brace yourself
for its low blows to the heart and soul
kneeling for the eight-count, if need be,
grabbing hold of proffered hands
from angels and kindred spirits

Gleanings from Gospels

Judge not that ye be not judged
said the donkey riding Jesus,
love thy neighbor, and let it go at that;
don't let thy left hand know
what thy right hand is doing,
and who, may I ask, has mastered *that* trick?
let whoever is without sin stand naked before us
so we may admire their cosmetic surgery;
if there are qualified stone throwers in this town
I have yet to meet them;
blessed are the peacemakers
though I have yet to meet them either;
beware of false prophets, for they're in the majority;
no man can serve two masters
and the pure of heart will serve neither;
give us this day our daily bread,
a pleasurable bed, and no fear of tomorrow;
knock and it shall be opened unto you,
knock twice and it will remain closed,
leaving doubters in their usual dither

Shadows Are Sufficient

Plato told the story
of shadows on the cave wall
cast by figures moving to and fro
in front of a roaring fire

we, ourselves, can't see those figures
nor can we see the fire,
we can only see the shadows
so, for us, that's all there is

indeed, our knowledge is illusion,
reflections of dancing images
with exaggerated aspects
more entertaining than the truth

these shadows are mysterious,
with voluminous symbolism, albeit
monochromatic and one dimensional
providing an intellectual comfort zone

shouldst we be flung down from this cave
we would surely be distraught
unless, of course, we had the fortune
to land with head in the sand

I Envy Dogs

I envy dogs
when I see one sprawled
with paws outstretched
and chin on the floor
in conscience-free comfort
tried it myself once
but found it quite awkward
not to mention inane
for why would a sane man
wish to emulate a canine
a lower form of life
a prancing buffoon
dimwitted servant
master of crass
cagey maybe, but clueless
relentless, however,
in pursuit of the pecking order
immune to the deflation of defeat
goddamn! I envy dogs

Questions Zinging

You look into my leftfield eyes
with questions zinging from your brow:
why do I spend my off-day evenings
preaching to the off-key choir?
don't I know the game is over
when the scoreboard runs out of zeros?
wherefore crave split-fingered power
with a deuce of diamonds up my sleeve?
will I swear upon my namesake's honor
my shifty nose was never shorter?
will I choose nightmares over barren slumber
insinuating to err is to fly?
I have no answers, just enhanced memories
of winning and losing by the suicide squeeze

Clyde

Dr. Jekyll was a nice guy
in every fathomable way,
endeared by his patients
for his genuine devotion
to their total well-being,
well respected by his peers
as a beacon of integrity
in the noblest profession,
adored by his genteel beloved
for his gallantry and warmth
with his name on every register
in the upper social strata
But, then again, there was his Hyde side
just like you and me, Clyde

Panhandlers Litany

Give all the bums a buck
to insure the worthy one-percent
will collect enough to journey through the night.
Met this guy in a yin-yang shirt proclaiming:
"The amount of evil in this world
is equal to the amount of good,
and that's all the equality there is in this world."
I said: "hmm" as I slipped this soothsayer a buck.
A smiling mime with a cardboard sign that read:
"Dare to live without a mirror!"
got an I-don't-think-so with his dollar.
A raggedy woman with a sad-eyed doggie tucked
under her arm accepted her buck with flair.
A brazen teen demanding bus fare, when asked
where she's going, smugly declared: "astray!"
as I dropped a buck into her eager palm.
A cool dude in a beret goes: "Spare some dough, bro?"
well, that worked, and he got himself a buck.
An ardent gent in a vintage suit walking along
with me, spieling politics, got a buck to go away.
A charming old lady in a floral bonnet winked
as she slipped my buck into her velvet purse.
A big man sitting on the sidewalk with a big cup
which he jingled towards me as I approached
received a donation that made no sound in his cup.
A man with a cane holding up his buck exclaimed:
"This will buy food for my kitty." So, I gave him
another, and implored him not to divulge its use.
While stopped for a traffic light I saw a peculiar
cardboard sign that asked: "Save the planet?
What for? No one enjoys living here anymore."
Still, my buck was snatched from my door.

An indignant fellow hollering over and over:
"Why is there a stop-sign on every corner?
not just the perilous, but *every* corner?"
to my blank stare bemoaned: "Mr. Hyde would know"
as his trembling hand pocketed my dollar.
Then a calm voice from beneath a fedora surmised:
"At least we got it right in the fifties, Jack."
"Hmm" I mused as I paid him his due.
Yes, give all the bums a buck
to insure the worthy one-percent
will collect enough to journey through the night.

What's So Fetching About Change?

What's so fetching about change?
asked the elderly gypsy lady
as she puffed on her Meerschaum pipe;
it receives such widespread veneration,
yet seems Puritanical to me;
you know, that sect that sailed
from England in search of
a new world to purify, and dropped
anchor and rancor upon Massachusetts,
home of friendly Indians who
showed them how to grow maize
and where to hunt game, all the while
being urged to give their thanks
to the Puritan god; next, those
friendly Quakers arrived, merely wishing
to plant seeds of peace;
but peace conflicts with purity
that's being forced upon the community
so they were soon banished,
migrating south to Providence
where they reaped bountiful harvests
of tolerance; and no one got hung

So, what's so fetching about change?
repeated the elderly gypsy lady;
does the desire spring from arrogance,
that *all* is within our power?
more likely it's from innocence
as we really do believe this world is *ours*

This elderly gypsy lady then proceeded
to spread a few cards on the table,

gazed at them for a few moments,
puffing rhythmically on her Meerschaum,
and casually declared to her audience:
these cards tell me truthfully today
the same things they've been telling
me and my ancestors for centuries,
don't you know; though we do
get to shuffle the deck,
said she, bemusedly

Cardboard Weaponry

Mobs on the march !
don't get in their way
you know the route they're taking
let them have their day

their cardboard signs contain
the latest righteous umbrage
expressed in clever slogans
with maladroit lettering

reveling in sheer numbers
oozing through the streets
the power of intimidation
adds swagger to their steps

vainly searching for meaning
in lives awash in abuse,
settling for a wink of fame when
their sign makes the evening news

That Thorny One-Percent

That thorny one-percent who,
for whatever reasons,
refrain from taking part in politics
bring on themselves the condemnation
of the other ninety-nine percent
who insist they have no right
to remain aloof from
the people's quest for power
and, though they're only one-percent,
their indifference tends to undermine
the urgency of democracy,
how dare they infer it to be folly !

Just Another Day

You know what they say
when the shit hits the fan
it pays to be an also-ran
as the front-runners get sprayed
while the stragglers still play
on their beat-up banjos
like it was just another day

Cahoots

Guess I'll go back
to where I was born
try and get in touch with my roots
I'm sure they'll know me
I still look the same
shabby clothes and fancy boots
I'm sure they'll be amused
when I tell 'em how I learned
fame and failure are in cahoots

Quest in Vain

Everybody looks the other way
as you furtively dry your tears
everybody offers you a prayer
with better-you-than-me sympathy

who do you trust to tell the truth
when you ask them if your head's on straight,
for when you take a good look in the mirror
your own Mr. Hyde is gazing back at you

your life has been a quest in vain
for that unholy grail of notoriety,
first rumored in your old neighborhood
where you brazenly gambled your innocence

quit complaining 'bout the days remaining
they're only coming at you one at a time,
try a new coat of paint on your cross
perhaps there's a "promised land" after all

Sufficiently Satisfied

There's a halo 'round the hanged man
and frosting on the communal host
the ghost has lost its memory
so the crow calls out the score
the last wisp of hope ascends
to merge with passing clouds
while the silver toting scapegoat
shares the bed of sleeping beauty;
now a hundred years or so go by
devoid of dreams and nightmares
one awakes, one doesn't try
being sufficiently satisfied;
"No sweeter sound than the death knell"
so they say outside of Hell

In Like a Lion, Out Like a Lullaby

March, for sure, is an inscrutable month
testing our faith in February's shadow
with wind chill voodoo, snow-white nor'easters
and frost-on-your-windshield encores

then, first day of spring, bud-a-bing !
night and day are equal
you and me are balanced
with a renewed sense of wonder

I see daffodils popping up through the snow
I see shamrocks in a thousand smiles
I hear Danny Boy sung in Japanese
I hear pipes of Pan in my dreams

indeed, coping with nature's dire transitions
sires lion-hearted resilience

Ripples and Dust

The oak tree by the pond
lets go of a November leaf
despite its turning brilliant gold;
but it doesn't descend
directly like an acorn,
powerless against gravity,
instead, it spirals with dips
and pirouettes, as though
mocking its fate, and
its soundless landing on the pond
still manages to produce ripples

Love can be given
then taken away, though
sometimes the caring remains;
while intimacy is denied,
a cloak of privy praise is bestowed,
a parachute with averted eyes,
turning falling into fluttering,
so the landing is thudless,
all the same, raising dust

How Do You Like Your Coffee?

Gliding down hallway
coffee cup filled to brim
piping hot !
with enticing aroma
fore and aft, when --
psycho-kitty-ambush !!!
coffee spills, spatters
and burns
ensuing swears & curses
loudest of the day !
kitty nonchalantly
lapping cooled version
from furthest puddle's edge,
finishes, glides away

Emerald Hero

Comic book good looks
too lean to be true
silk jacket, leather jeans
rapscallion poser
set free in the bright

rock & roll shaman
casting fusion spells
causing widespread shivers
bit Hendrix, bit Smokey,
bit Presley, all Dublin

crooning legends of tragedy
counts himself living proof
wielding power of the prophets
incited by its possession
with melancholy majesty

hardcore mates on board
home sweet home on the brink
"some of us won't survive"
trying to get a handle on hope
available less than you think

Undisputed

There was a time
when the boxer who became the undisputed
heavyweight champion of the world
was known to everyone. Admired by majority,
envied even, though despised by some,
yet respected by all.
He was the alpha male of the pack !
He had emerged from the local gym scene
to enter the fray of spartan wannabees,
climbing the ladder into top ten rankings,
that prestigious domain of the "contenders".
Then fought them all, one by one, until
there was only the champ remaining,
soon to be ex-champ, entitled to a re-match,
followed by "hanging them up for good".
The new champ gets to pose on the pedestal
for as long as he can dispose of his challengers,
until one disposes of him. And so it goes.

There was a time
when society mirrored the sport of boxing.
True, 'twas not an age of affluence,
nonetheless, the populace was frisky and cocky
with rakish fedoras to prove it, and
a genial challenge in every eye,
yet, respect ran rampant !

Anti-Gratitude

Humans are wont to thank
somebody or something whenever
life is good, or
things go as planned;
for some it's a deity,
for others the universe;
but now in these times
when government is god
it's the posers in power
with images anointed
on magazine covers

by the same token,
when things don't go well
someone must be blamed,
even cursed and showered
with animosity and venom,
thus freeing the populace
from any complicity

yet, there are precocious individuals
who dare pat themselves on the back
when things go as planned,
and, dutifully, look in the mirror
when faced with failures;
indeed, I'm pleased you're one of them

Veneration of Neptune

O mighty Neptune, god of the immense Sea,
we venerate thee; for thou art ruler
over three-quarters of our planet's
sprawling territory and, most likely,
three-quarters of its life, as well

so, tell me, Neptune,
do you control this Sea totally?
or are you like the lion-tamer
with his whip and his chair
who maneuvers the lion into
grudgingly performing those droll routines
while risking his life every time?

what magic is in your trident
whereby you goad the Sea into ferocity
then calm it down into blue tranquility?
and is your own life on the line every time?

we humans act most wisely when
dealing with the Sea, as we recognize
its power lies well beyond our domain;
so, we learn all we can about its moods
and foibles, its benevolence when desiring
to balance its mayhem; and are content
to keenly master its navigation

would that we could be so wise onshore . . .

The Pendulum

The pendulum swings back and forth,
back and forth, back and forth,
the pendulum swings back and forth
and it's taking me for a ride

pranced right through the fifties
on a leash of law and order
yet, enjoyed getting away with
everything I shouldn't oughta

spiraled through the sixties
as religion ceased to rule
truth was transition
and beauty favored the fool

now, the pendulum swings
away from merriment and laughter
though you might slow it down
in a nearby bar
with a glass of rye and water
but not for long, as

clouds turn stormy when
the wind has its way
charcoal gray in the midst of winter
the Banshee cries,
a dear friend dies
and you curse the Fates that sent her

when straights get dire
you might gaze into fire
and pray to one who owes a favor

should they stand and deliver
an arrow to your quiver
you'll have power to be your own savior

The pendulum swings back and forth,
back and forth, back and forth,
the pendulum swings back and forth
and I'm heading for the "other" side

Haikus: "All Too Human"

A squeal of laughter
coming from the infant's crib
your own Bethlehem

Sunny day, strolling
around the old neighborhood
blithesome rainy eyes

Spirited fiddles !
packed house at weekly seisiun
-- sipping my Guinness

Gliding to bus stop
under open umbrella
pitter-patter day

A fork in the road
trudging multitudes don't split
-- praying for courage

Sideswiped a parked car
running late, no witnesses
-- prized guest of honor

Bandito hiding
poised to flip on flashing lights
-- mom's day is ruined

Peculiar shadow
unlit candle flickering
-- empty wine bottle

Veggie burgers soothe
pangs of the belly, and blues --
sweet potato fries

Eight months of training
finishes first marathon
-- the kids want ice cream

Painting the bedroom
mellow colors for sweet dreams
-- Dali over bed

Thanksgiving dinner
twelve smiles around the table
-- hope for humans yet

2. Jagged Stories

Salvation Park

While strolling through Salvation
Park late at night in a tranquil
rain with my beat-up umbrella in
one hand and my hand-me-down
clay pipe in the other emitting
an aroma best kept undercover

I came upon a pair of tapered candles
ensconced in chianti wine bottles
a few feet apart across the walkway
burning unattended with steady
defiant flames and felt a slight chill
as I was passing between them

encountered a personage on a bench
who nodded in my direction
with a non-committal expression
on the face and not a stitch
of clothing on the body, just
a big diamond on the middle finger

further along glimpsed a lithesome
couple in the shadows groping tenderly
with all four hands moving choreo-
graphically within day-glo gloves
from one to the other's front and back
privacies, uplifted faces glistening

next, stood before the statue of a soldier
from the war-to-end-all-wars who
claims he's been killed in every war
before or since, yet prefers to be

photographed as period art, rather
than as a factor in the farce, then

glanced at a trash barrel encased in a stylish
wrought iron frame and spotted this morning's
newspaper right at home midst the mound of
casually strewn nips and cups
with its partially visible headline proclaiming
something about some hooker hitting powerball

now cutting across the grass for a closer look
at the local garden club's display of gently
swaying cosmos and lavender cleomes
lovingly arranged 'round an antique lamppost, when
I felt a sharp pain between the shoulder blades
and saw my shadow welcoming me

but the pain soon faded into rapture and
while lying prostrate on the soft greenery with
a knife in my back and an empty back pocket
where my wallet used to be, I recalled the
naked personage on the bench and thought:
there but for the grace of God goes me

The Tower of Allure

The gambler inhales on the riverboat
intently circling the murky moat
surrounding the Tower of Allure
with six windows and no door
an erection of unknown stone
five maidens and Death call it home
switching rooms every night
much to Death's dark delight
as the windows are mirrors
that lay bare one's desires
and each sorceress dispenses
charms to thrill his senses

The gambler has rope and a plan
though an imprudent prisoner of Pan
with a deathwish he wishes to nurse
while he rendezvous with each maiden first
understanding the rules of the game
in this tower devoid of all blame
six ways leading in and no exit out
the shrewd gambler disguises his doubt
nimbly climbing to room Number Four
in his dreams he has been there before
his reflection beaming in the glass
the madness of a man soon to pass
now preening in the face of the fates
as the kiss of Death duly awaits . . .

In a Fog

I was in a fog in the fog
on a restless summer night
when my footsteps fortook me
all the way to Derby Light
as I was approaching
the end of the pier
I found Elias Derby
hanging out there
he said: you're fair to middlin'
as a merchant, matey,
but you'll never be
a carefree millionaire
in a fog in the fog

saw a white elephant walking
on the windowpane water
he was heading downtown
where they're seeking a savior
met Blackbeard the Pirate
I could hardly recognize him
for his hair was full of sparkles
and an angel stood beside him
in a fog in the fog

heard a sweet voice humming
a tune I used to know
said her name was Bridget
used to live here long ago
came across an albatross
perched upon a pole
he winked at me and whispered:

you might enjoy growing old
in a fog in the fog

now there's a monster in the fog
impersonating God
passing judgment on your song
claims you got it all wrong
but there's a message in the fog
from the prince who was a frog
if you're lucky you may feel it
before the monster comes to steal it
in a fog in the fog

and there I go again
in a fog in the fog

The Godly Power of Vengeance
   (musings on Melville's gospel)

Ahab was a peerless captain,
a master of the winds and currents,
who knew the oceans like
the streets of his neighborhood

in his cabin with his maps
spread across the oaken table
he could chart the migrations
of all the whales in the world

but his scrutiny was fixated
on the conceivable whereabouts
of the lone *white* whale
among the million blue and black

such odds might seem diminutive
to the wagering public
without the means to calculate
the godly power of vengeance

that might be evenly possessed
by both man and whale, though
Ahab believed he was fated to be
the slayer of that demon leviathan

now, he could be surprisingly
compassionate when it didn't involve
straying from his course, but cold-
hearted as King Herod when it did

our great planet seems dwindled

to those oft sailing round it,
the hunt for a solitary less daunting
with only four oceans for evasions

indeed, Captain Ahab found his whale
in the largest of the oceans
and got close enough to harpoon him,
the penultimate high of scorning God's plan

for the harpoon is the vital connection
between the whalers and the whale
shifting the odds to the whalers
in the normal scheme of things

but the white whale proved to be
fated, himself, to foist upon Ahab
more havoc than he could heed, singing
the same refrain: vengeance is mine !

as the whale, too, was determined
to end Ahab's unflagging bitterness,
first taking his leg, then his life, along
with his ship and once-innocent crew

oh, the tragedy in the winds
is the twist of fate of said crew
who were stalwart in their mission
before acquiescing to iniquity

it seems faith is man's weakness
when it overpowers his reason
allowing folly the opportunity
to become the preferable option

so these whalers handed over
their faith to their captain,
who was cogently strewing
visions of doubloons

such leaders prone to madness
brandish arcane ingenuity,
beguiling their followers
into craving their own doom

yet, the sea gods ease off
and release a lone whaler
who then struggles to reconcile
his good fortune with his guilt

having seen the light from the depths,
but stripped of shipmates, he must
distance himself from vengeance
if he's ever to shrink the void

Creation Redux

Nuclear explosion, mammoth devastation
human technology, safety test bungled
uncontrollable fires, widespread radiation
humans evacuated, animals flee
thousand mile exclusion zone installed

eventually, fires burn out
followed by eerie stillness --
time goes by ...

as it turns out, plant life
little affected by the radiation
beyond the fire zone, not only
surviving, but burgeoning,
and surrounding forest thickens

next, a red deer is calmly
nibbling on the expansive greenery,
and he's not alone --
as other large mammals
are moving into the area
with tidings spreading by
vibes and songs:
though the air's a bit iffy
the food is plentiful and
graze where you choose;
before long come elk, wild boar, bear;
and rare breeds of horses thought to be extinct;
then wolves with their shiny fur coats
and jeweled eyes that sparkle so
when roaming with abandon --
no two-legged nemeses here

then the beavers arrive
and begin damming the rivers,
overflowing to form marshlands,
soon home to blackbirds
swaying on cattails, and
their myriad feathered cousins,
plus waterfowl honking their delight
mid wildflowers of vibrant colors,
a peaceful milieu of beauty and song !

only thing missing is *us*
in this woodland haven,
serendipitously spawned
through artless errors;
and by dint of wilderness justice
we alone are unable to adapt
to the environs we've tainted

thus, a contented animal kingdom
flourishes within said exclusion zone,
with only humans excluded;
and one might surmise:
the gods got it right the second time

A Messenger by Happenstance

Once upon a ship at sea
a raven flew into my dream
inviting me to an island home
he shares with souls set free

from bodies visually challenged
expunged by their own hand
voluntary brutalities
mortifying next of kin

said raven travels 'tween the worlds
of spirit and of flesh and bone
a messenger by happenstance
who tends to crow in riddles:

if beauty lies in beholder's eyes
doth truth protest too much?
when Satan sits in judgement
might he see you as a prize?

why is deprivation bitter
when no deeper than one's greed?
is there cruelty in the heart
inflicting pain upon the mirror?

wherefore this beguiling voice
coyly crooning in my ear
water water in the lungs
should nirvana be your goal?

now behold this ship of dreamers
on the sea of premonitions

with sails full and moon likewise
indifferent to the dawn

spirits visible in the fog
a raven perches on our prow
we turn without the captain's order
lo, who filled in tomorrow's log?

Orbit of Oblivion

Have you ever seen a gliding eagle
struck in mid-air by the blade of a windmill?
well, when it hits the ground, boyo,
this magnificent bird is dead on arrival !
but, no one owns him
so no one mourns him;
unless, there's a mate and chickies
awaiting his return with victuals,
eventually accepting the actuality
he's never coming back to them;
and, perhaps, they share misgivings,
was it they who drove him away?
adding guilt to their dismay;
lo, the gloomy mate still has her instincts
and goes in search of food, herself;
life goes on, the world still turns,
the windmill's propeller still spins
in its orbit of oblivion . . .

Farewell, Bid the Crow

Come gather round ladies, I bring a message from Hell
cried the crow on the balcony of their elegant hotel,
with your wealth and your servants you travel first
class
but for some of you tomorrow will not come to pass;
to your masquerade this evening comes a guest with
no disguise
whom no one can describe, beyond Death was in his
eyes

But, they turned a deaf ear to the voice of the crow
dismissed him as a fool with no place to go
just a jester, a prankster, how could he know their
fate?
farewell, bid the crow, I'm afraid it's too late

Come gather round hunters, I bring a message from
Hell
for the fox you are chasing has a story to tell,
he's a beast reincarnate from a century ago
when your ancestors pillaged the village below;
now you follow him madly down through this ghost
town
where your ravaged remains will never be found

But, they turned a deaf ear to the voice of the crow

Come gather round strangers, I bring a message from
Hell
to warn you of the dangers lurking down in your well,
when you draw up your bucket with the water of life
better taste it yourself before giving to your wife;

for, lo and behold, as the moon starts to wane
your heart will stop beating, though your pain will
remain

But, they turned a deaf ear to the voice of the crow

Come gather round clergy, I bring a message from Hell
they'll be coming for your souls at the tolling of the
bell,
for your vows have been broken so blatantly often
your bones will never know the warmth of a coffin;
so dust off your bibles and search through your verses
for just the right reference to justify your curses

Ah, but they started to listen to the voice of the crow
though he may be a fool, he seems to know where
they'll go
and he *might* just be the one who determines their fate,
so they crucified that crow out by the front gate,
indeed, they nailed him to a cross and sat back to wait;
but, farewell, bid the crow, I'm afraid it's too late,
too late, too late, too late, too late . . .

Suckers for a Sideshow

(We're all rubes in search of a rainbow
which makes us suckers for a sideshow . . .)

After P.T. Barnum retired from politics
he joined with Bailey in the circus business,
he'd danced with power but longed to kiss wealth.
Though his "sucker born every minute"
saying wasn't his own profundity,
he did make it infamous, and
we suckers line up continually
to prove it obvious

As a politician he'd mastered the art
of manipulating the masses with rhetoric
and merely transferred this mastery
to the parallel theatre of illusion
for as every astute promoter notes
it's the frosting that sells the cake, while
its chocolate interior enamors the customer
who returns for more, and grants a good score;
so, too, in the circus game, death-defying derring-do
gives the thrill seekers their money's worth,
while sideshow promos bring 'em in the door

Tom Thumb, world's smallest man, was his biggest
hit, until he hit upon "the mermaid," which brought
human myopia out of Plato's cave and into
the religion of fanatic impressionism

Now Barnum was a con-artist extraordinaire,
with a flair for flaunting it boldly, yet
his shows got five-star ratings, as the falsehoods

that seduced us into venturing within were forgiven
quite readily, once we were transported to
the drama of the high wire, the fools without a net,
the clowns without a conscience, not to mention
killer cats, nimble bears, eveready doggies and,
of course, acrobat families from foreign lands

But, "the mermaid" topped them all! the only one
in captivity was the claim! for who could swear
they'd ever seen another on land or at sea?
he painted the town with pen and ink flyers
hyped it haughtily in the national media
hawked it fervently with evangelical barkers
now, who could miss this beatific opportunity?
the lines were longer than one could remember
as we waited impatiently for our turn to gander
only to be blindsided with disbelief, as the mermaid
was only a monkey! a monkey with fins attached
somehow 'neath her dress, albeit neatly done,
and we all walked out in mass protest, incensed!
while Barnum chirped to Bailey: they'll be back.

And, true enough, next day most returned
for another look, and brought friends along with us,
and those friends returned with more friends
for the chance to see the one and only mermaid
in captivity, and we could say we saw it and you
didn't, oh ye of little faith, and after a while,
we did see it!

The second viewing proved to be the turning point
as it looked a little less like a monkey, and a little
more like the mermaid we so badly wanted it to be,
and by the third viewing the monkey had dis-

appeared altogether, and we saw only "a mermaid"
who now appeared as lovely on stage as she was
in our dreams; yea, all present shared this joy
and went home believing dreams do come true
and, P.T. Barnum, we believe in you!

Opportunities on a Side Street (a trilogy)

I. Redistribution

We were strolling downtown
on a mid-September eve
turning left onto the side street
leading to our favorite local pub
serving hardy no-frills fare
with tonight's specials beckoning
and a window table waiting

when up ahead we chance to witness
a man slumping to the pavement
with two other men standing
alongside, but ignoring him
as they rifle through his wallet
from which they remove a wad
as thick as the Sunday paper

then nod to us as we approach
and slip us each a hundred,
adding: enjoy your evening, folks,
and remember, you saw nothing;
whence they casually walk away,
while we decide to pass on the local pub
and head uptown to a jazz joint

II. Redistribution, With Style

A mugging goes down on 3rd Street,
injuries inflicted, jackpot extracted from victim

with masters-of-the-trade efficiency;
a little while later, over on 8th Street,
in mixed-bag neighborhood pub,
Jimmy and Rudy buying rounds for the table,
a good time being had by all;
when girl scout cookie peddlers come by
they each buy five boxes, so
everyone present goes home with one;
on his way back from men's room
Jimmy drops a few bills into the worthy-
cause canister on the bar, Rudy
visits booth where Mrs. Muldoon
is still mourning loss of husband Kevin,
expresses his condolences once again,
while slipping her next month's rent;
Jimmy and Rudy say goodnight to all
and head off to Bruins game; Mrs. Muldoon
and neighbor agree: they're such nice boys;
neighbor asks what they do for a living,
and Mrs. Muldoon replies she wasn't sure,
but they sure do dress with style, don't they?

III. Homeless Virtue

Homeless couple gazing down
at body of man laid out
on 3rd Street sidewalk,
breathing, but bleeding,
and ain't going nowhere;
a search of his clothes
reveals wallet is missing, so
with address not readily knowable

return his house keys to his pocket,
taking only his cell phone
and a Snickers bar which
they pass back and forth
as they stroll on down the street,
nibbling to make it last;
a safe distance away
they dial 911 and call for
an ambulance: there's an
emergency on 3rd Street !

The man awakes in the
emergency ward of the
mile-away hospital, with
a bandage on his head
and a blur in his brain;
he doesn't know what happened
and probably never will,
but still has his house keys,
so he still has his house,
just knows he's beholden
to someone, which someone
has just fenced his phone
in a bar over on 8th Street

Witnessed by None

Turning the pages
in a book of lies
I observed
through squinty eyes
what appeared to be
a glint of truth
a veritable account
of a peculiar incident
witnessed by none
other than myself
which led me to surmise
the life that ended
that night transcended
the normal journey
to the cemetery
summoning the wherewithal
to have visited
(surely unsolicited)
the author of this book
I now despise
while one might query
is your witness
in this theory
a promising perpetrator,
has-been hallucinator,
or banshee fairy
who could care less,
otherwise?

Ode to Orneriness

He should've been
an alley cat
but ended up with me
on the top flat
of a three-decker
with a bird's eye view
of the seaside neighborhood;
he was Beau from birth
striped gray with attitude
and orneriness who
would hiss for hello
and howl for the thrill
of shattering tranquility,
who abused my rules
made rags of my clothes,
who guarded his yard
against naïve trespassers
of his own feline persuasion,
harassed the poor mailman
disdained gourmet food
consigned milk to mice,
yet, welcomed the sandman
and basked in love from the ladies
upon whose laps he'd purr
in his skull-and-crossbones collar,
tossing a jeering wink my way . . .

But, clandestinely the Reaper
slipped in this afternoon
and tonight I'm downright
ornery, and raging
against the tranquility !

This Mystic Mountain

Anxious Patrick disembarked in Ireland
as a missionary with the requisite zeal
on a venture to convert Pagan peasants
into righteous stalwart Christians

said peasants were a superstitious lot
attuned to charms and potions
for protection, and good fortune
in love and lust and cures and such,

who coexisted with a Faerie realm
indigenous to this emerald isle,
where their magic flourished in the mist,
with shapeshifting their forte

now, Celtic gods were known to reside
on a holy mountain in Mayo
with peasant villages situated
in line with sun-rays from the summit

rather brazenly, Patrick did
climb this mystic mountain,
spending forty days and nights upon it
in meditation and in prayer

but, all the while, arcane premonitions
as thick as the enduring mist
percolate into his subconscious
causing Patrick to reassess his plan

whence, his purifying notion of banishing
gave way to a system of blending

Pagan mores and favored talismans
with Christian prayers of forgiveness

thereupon, he descended the mountain
whistling a tune he'd heard every night
in dreams of himself nimbly dancing
midst a circle of glistening mushrooms

wearing a native charm, the shamrock,
Patrick now travels the countryside
preaching his blended gospel,
while the Faeries look the other way

A Church Fair

Came upon a church fair
on a rainy morning first
week in December
on our way to somewhere
in county Clare

impressive were the offerings
local artesian wrought
along with the opportunity
to sample teas and breads
following preliminary tour of hall

after which I returned
to the batik booth
in the back-left corner
manned by Vivien from Kinvara
portraying flowers primarily

but I'd glimpsed a lone faerie
upon a rock midst the wildflowers
on the first trip through
and now had time to gander,
while Vivien uncovered another

"I've got this multiple one I just
finished last night" she said,
"which hasn't been hemmed yet
so I can't hang it, but
tell me what you think of it . . ."

so, now I've got this curious batik
hanging on my bedroom wall
and every night I enjoy a pint
this motley band of faeries comes
traipsing through my dreams !

Banshee Blues

I met this woman on the train
with hair more black than midnight rain
eyes pale green like the moss on a cross
and features etched from cathedral glass
I was studying her trying to guess her age
as she was turning another page
in her notebook full of names and dates
with notations how they met their fate
I said looks like we're in for pleasant weather
in your hat is that a raven feather?
I'm going to the mountains on holiday
my favorite place to get away

her flashing eyes cut short my story
her sweet voice now turned rather chilling
when she said ye shan't find any glory
in a death that isn't self-fulfilling
that night ye stood all alone on the edge
after all yer fair-weather friends had fled
with that dark cloud hovering above yer head
'til ye woke up trembling in yer soaking wet bed
why do ye think ye were spared, ye fool?
ye should be gone now, ye know the rule
ye simply were given a second chance
so have one more drink now before ye dance
then she walked away on down the aisle
as the train slowed down to round a bend
she looked back once with the hint of a smile
and I never saw her face again
yes, I never saw her face again

I've climbed the holy mountain on a foggy afternoon

where Pagans and Christians before me have tread
with all of us seeking to find the right tune
for when comes our turn to dance with the dead
I've seen the sun go down upon the bay
a thousand times now since that day
when the Banshee vanished from the train
but I'm looking over my shoulder just the same
for I can feel her eyes on a stormy night
when lightning finds me in the shadow
and I can hear her cry in the howling wind
as I pray that I'll live to see tomorrow

then she walked away on down the aisle
as the train slowed down to round a bend
she looked back once with the hint of a smile
and I never saw her face again
yes, I never saw her face again
until tonight . . .

Our Man's Grin

I climbed out of bed at 6:30am
as I do on most mornings
(but this was not just another day)
went on downstairs to greet
the dawn and let kitty out
to collude with nature,
with clouds covering up
nine-tenths of the sky, leaving
only an oval of blue, in the center
of which shining brightly
was a solitary star, the last
star of the evening, the
Morningstar, usually known
as the planet Venus, symbol
of love on most days
(but this was not just another day)
as today we mourn a love lost

aye, the most beloved member
of our local public house kinship
has suddenly dastardly departed
from the land of woe, leaving the rest
of us high and dry moaning it can't be!
beset with angry vulnerability,
for the Reaper is cruelest
when he steals from the top
of one's pyramid of friends

so, clad in deferential black
we go to the church to sing
the hymns, chew the host,
and shake the hands for peace,

with the priest turning out to be
a decent singer, himself, and his
poignant sermon gratefully comprising
no more than beginning, middle, end

as the service concludes and the
procession down the aisle
commences, I behold the tenor
and guitarist giving it hell
up there in the choir loft
singing a Christy Moore lament
sounding holier than Christmas
wrenching the anger from our gut
causing more grown men to cry
than I've ever seen before
and as I watch them through
my own tears which are rolling
freely down my cheeks and
landing where they may,
for it's purging water, and
will not stain the church pew nor
my dusted-off suit,
I recall the Morningstar
glowing after the moon had retired
and before the sun had risen,
alerting me to the likelihood that,
going forward, whenever
engaging in pub-style folderol,
we'll be mindful of
our man's grin of approval

Ride on, John Casey, ride on . . .

Haikus: Unfettered

Fox knows hideaways
on both sides of the river
hounds can bark all day

Mockingbird fears cat --
but, when chicks are in the nest
cat fears mockingbird

Leader of the pack
shan't talk his way to the top
-- wisdom of wolfdom

Forsythias burst !
yellow favorite color --
for the next few weeks

Choir sings in the street
light rain becomes heavier
all but one disperse

Lovers get naked --
just gazing at each other
suffices tonight

He ran for office
declined all contributions
lone integrity

Power of the herd
fiercest in a mad stampede --
jackrabbit is doomed

Almost 5pm
they'll be home any minute --
dog lays by the door

Resounding tapping
coming from one of those trees
can't spot the redhead

Raucous crowd in pub
no bouncers hovering here
-- anarchism rules well

Made right decisions
then, too, made wrong decisions
-- bribed the scorekeeper

3. The Scales of Fortuity

Wind Shifts

You chase the carrot
chase the carrot
chase the carrot
so close yet
so far away
you chase the carrot
chase the carrot
chase the carrot
wind shifts and
you put it away

There Is No Road

I am alone
here in my mind
there is no map
and there is no road
it's Celtic knotwork
just as yours is
and no -- I won't trade

What's He Thinking?

Gaggle of grackles
ravenous sparrows
descend upon my lawn
to picnic on
the seeds laid out
that very morn
just takes one bird
to spread the word
as far as
two woods over
now bumping
into one another
chirping burping
no one looking
slinking
into the yard
black-patched white cat
from the 'hood
good times to be had
in stalking mode
along the fence
low to ground
sans any sound
eyes transfixed
on the feathers
he settles into crouch position
a bounding leap
from the bevy
and he stares
thirty seconds
without blinking
what's he thinking?

is he choosing?
instead
he whispers "meow"
birds in panic
scatter to trees !
black-patch turns
saunters away
nefariously pleased

Urgency I Dread

Puckish kitty dancing on my head
with that urgency I dread
well before the hour
I rise from this bed

but, look - look - look -
look - look she said
so I opened my eyes
and beheld the *dawn*
blazing through the trees mergatroyd red !

ensuing silence eventually tempered
by a hoarsely whispered: yowsa !
it's so good to be not dead

and as for thee, bold kitty,
thou shalt now be fed

My Tenth Martini

Regiment of starlings
lined up on a wire
serenading incessantly
in a conductorless choir

kitty on the sidewalk
absorbed in fervent prayer:
"just let me fly
this one time, Lord,
and we'll be dancing in the street
in sublime pantomime
to the tune of falling feathers
with my pick of the sopranos"

now, as I drain my tenth martini
my kitty soars above me

In the Realm of the Pub

An infant in a pub
being rocked upon his mama's knee
at a table full of musicians
playing wild Irish tunes
is wide-eyed and all ears,
being introduced to the bliss
shared by this motley gathering of
jolly imbibers and gabbers;
he remains quiet, with no desire to
compete with the music
and tall tales, astutely ascertaining
in the realm of the pub
his smiles aren't the only thing
to set the big folks aflutter

A Basket of Fruitless Remedies

Set 'em up, bartender
for all the earlybirds at the bar
how 'bout a toast to tardiness
my destination ain't too far
got a left-for-dead limo
and my driver waits outside
calls herself Miss Joy Deville
a better lover than a guide

set 'em up, bartender
I've got a winning hand to spend
wish I could remember
which greeting I should send:
congratulations? sympathy?
bon voyage? have tea with me?
maybe I'll send them all
in a basket of fruitless remedies

set 'em up, bartender
I'm really on a roll
stick this in your blender
and view the colors of your soul:
your blues may offer silver linings
your greens may shade your eyes
while your rose parade gets rained on
under obfuscating skies

set 'em up, bartender
I've got the urge to perform
fill my glass just one more time
and I'll sing a gospel song
if you didn't know by now

Jesus hired a Leprechaun
to hide the path to Paradise
from those who fail to bring a rhyme along

Roses in the Mud

Annual "run for the roses"
speakers blaring Elvis
singing "Kentucky Rain"
(one gets prescient in one's grave)
and rain it does

electric horses single file
close-cropped manes sleek
just brushed tails still
driven riders calm
hardknocks graduates in
satin and leather
poise on parade
but drama percolating:
wide-brimmed festooned fans pose
wide-eyed ticket clutchers buzz
hatless guy with orange tie
flamboyantly bet a *hundred grand*
now stands alone looking smug --
handily, starting gate being filled
hundred thousand breaths being held
post time !

muddy track shuffles deck
fearless favorites no less frisky
but hoofs compete with hearts today
three year olds in prime
jockeys seen it all
they're off !

number 4 breaks out first
grabs the rail

no big deal at time
it seems, as others
pass him by outside
claiming lead, setting pace
while 4 is cruising
clinging shadow
shaving distance
saving pistons
primed for second explosion
far turn, moment of truth
makes his move
splits frontrunners, grabs lead
needs no blinders
never looks back
relishes lustful whipping
wants it, smells it, wins it !

then we have
hatless guy with orange tie
jumping up and down
flapping arms like a duck
(only his smugness flies away)
winning ticket in his teeth
crazed exuberance in his eyes --
cameras return to the horses . . .

postscript:
a rich fool becomes richer
a noble horse becomes a legend

Planetary Hierarchy

The osprey perches
on the edge of his nest
made of branches, not of twigs,
a short distance from the shore
and gazes into space,
occasionally looking left for a while,
then right for a bit, not seeming to
focus on anything in particular;
perhaps musing on tonight's
fresh fillet dinner,
while I take his picture . . .
after which, go on my
grateful way; a glance
back over my shoulder
reveals he's not glancing
back at me; now, I wonder,
was he even aware I was there?
though I mightn't have been
close up, I was plainly visible
in this open marsh, and my
excitement must have sent
vibrations his way, as I assume
they're tuned into that sort
of thing; but his refusal
to acknowledge my lowly
presence conceivably indicates
his superior status in our
planetary hierarchy; after all,
he can fly !
ah, but I did capture
his imperious profile . . .

StringRiders

Five ladies on violins in a seisiun
whose eyes happen to close in unison
are transported to five flights of fancy:

the first goes back to this morning
watching the sun rise through the trees
as she sips her perfect tea
on her deck with her kitty perched
casually on the railing, pondering

the second is rocking her angel
in his cradle, while once again thanking
the faeries for not absconding with
her bonnie melody, and leaving in his place
a bundle of sniggering dissonance, yet
burning a bit of sage, just in case

number three is pedaling her bicycle
across the telephone wire, merrily
on her way to the office oblivious
to the endless traffic jam below, while
nodding to a passing crow

the fourth is musing a rendezvous
after the seisiun is spent, before
this eve evaporates, furtively licking her lips
while adding deft touches of melody
but tapping her boots à la galloping

the last one's lover has left her
and her bow is heavy with woe
drifting through old prison ruins

finds herself gradually accelerating
with anger rumbling inside her, glimpsing
lightning beyond the barred windows
hence her manic stroking drives
this band she's usually following

Four gents round out the combo
bouzouki, two flutes, and a banjo
at one with their pints on the table
providing a suitable landing for
returning beaming StringRiders
ready for a pint now, themselves

A Seasoned Panache

Observed this woman
of an age similar to my own
with the most striking crowsfeet
resembling Celtic knotwork
streaming from hazel eyes,
so delicately etched
into her trim profile
which gave her countenance
a seasoned panache
that captivated me
as I sat next to her,
one stool over, having turned
our backs to the bar,
using it now as a backrest,
while taking in the trad music
being improvised before us,
musing how subtle beauty
rewards the meandering eye, and
she must have sensed
the warm rays from my gaze
for her own eyes turned kindly
towards me and I could see
they retained the sparkle of youth
as she proceeded to clink
her glass to mine . . .

Let's Ride This Cloud

That leery look
in your alluring eyes
tells me you're wondering
who I am inside
beneath the mask
behind the wall
beyond the mirage
I'm not so tall
but I assure you
I'll amuse you
might infuse you
won't refuse you
the unusual
don't it seem like déjà vu
when the crowd roared?
climb on board
let's ride this cloud
to a carnival

thunder warned me
I ignored it
lightning struck me
didn't report it
lift me to heaven
drop me in hell
meet me at midnight
by the wishing well
I'm ablaze
in a daze
and night is falling
angels in shadows
are calling

my name in vain
as I just gaze at you
dancing in the rain
thunder warned me
I ignored it
lightning struck me again
I absorbed it

My Heart Blinks

I am going
where hope's alive
and dread is dead,
no need for blankets
on your bed,
where no one cares
where you came from
and no one minds
when you bang your drum
in the middle of the night !

I am going
where birds will perch
upon your hat
while lazy cat naps
on your lap,
where big dogs prance
round their front yards,
and gypsies with
their tarot cards
say the future looks so bright !

I am going
where faith is strong
despair's nowhere,
splintered sunlight
streaks your hair,
where lavish gardens
line the roads
and no one minds
when you pluck a rose
and plunk it in your bosom !

I am going
where chefs will croon
with spoon in hand
while old folks swoon
to funky band,
where glasses clink
on the balcony
and my heart blinks
when you declare to me:
never noticed you're so handsome !

I am going . . . I am gone !

A Free Town

P-town is a free town
one can feel it in the air
two can feel it holding hands, so
we crossed the bridge to cast down

dying wishes to the sea as planned
where the redeeming surf
with its omnipotent undertow
dispensed them 'round Neptune's heaven

we next uncork a bottle of schemes
and toast the genie within
turn our backs on propriety
and proceed to dupe reality:

   sunsets freeze-frame
   rainbows ricochet
   steeples, towers, flags and flowers
   serious galleries' artsy auras
   winking boutiques of Eros
   trios writhing to reggae
   queenies crooning karaoke
   darlings tippling lemon brewsies
   fogeys playing the fool with flair

closing time nudges us out the door
legless revelers giggle on home
in our minds we dupe posterity

Savoring Salty Deeds

One crutch is better than two
Pegleg Jacques swears it's true
lets you keep your hook hand free
to scoop whate're is tempting you

two weapons are better than one
a lesson learned while on the run
to live to toast oneself anew
hoisting a jar of the king's own rum

one park bench is all you need
to drift into those favored dreams
of voyages from long ago
bloody drowning in salty deeds

mates who've trawled the world for booty
posses the map to slumber's rev'rie

Love in a Salem Cemetery

A Jolly Roger's tattooed on her left arm
and just the word "Paradise" on her right,
she likes to make love in the cemetery
with the Morningstar burning bright

wears a heart-shaped silver locket
with the Reaper's image inside,
there's a rolled-up map in her pocket
and she sails on the morning tide

met her at The House of Seven Gables
wearing a t-shirt with a scarlet-A
and bemused by this wily fellow
with a touch of silver in his beard

soon offered to buy me a beverage
at the pub just down the street
where the shaven-head bartender
did greet her with a cordial wink

told me her name was Rebecca
as she nursed her Morgan on-the-rocks,
in a past life she'd been a smuggler
well known in notorious ports

claimed she's privy to buried treasure
while producing a wooden doubloon;
I, in turn, recited a poem about
the pelican who swallowed a whale

well, we closed the bar, and didn't get far
when she turned to me and said:

I feel our paths have crossed before
and I'm sure they will again

then she kissed me warmly on the lips
and I felt the fire within
as she led me to the cemetery, saying:
my love, it's time to sin

she chose the headstone of the hanging judge
to bear witness to our affair
and didn't seem to mind the chill
in the misty autumn air

she just lay there sparkling nekkid
with feral defiance in her eyes
and I didn't know good from evil,
I just knew I was on her side

a Jolly Roger's tattooed on her left arm
and just the word "Paradise" on her right,
she likes to make love in the cemetery
with the Morningstar burning bright

wears a heart-shaped silver locket
with the Reaper's image inside,
there's a rolled-up map in her pocket
and she sails on the morning tide

Joseph Spooner's Swansong

Joseph Spooner stood before
the freestanding full-length mirror
situated in the corner by the closet
of his uncluttered bedroom
and he grinned at his reflection
showing an aged man, fit and trim

Joseph had enjoyed his life on earth
for going on ninety-three years
and considered that number to be
one of momentous significance
since he set it as his ultimate goal
thirty-three years previous

he agreed with the traditional view
of life as a three-act play
and these acts in his own estimation
lasting about thirty years or so
comprising youth, adult, and elder,
with "ninety" a completed story

by then one's trusty bag of tricks
is pretty well depleted
with any years that follow
to be considered "curtain calls"
Joseph's good fortune tallied him
three such calls, and he was grateful

he knew well the legend of the Swansong
in which the swan goes silently through life
before breaking out into rapturous song
just before dying; and he chose to emulate

that celebratory ending, although
his own life was not known for its silence

he knew the term "swansong" came to mean
one's final performance before retirement
and proceeded to orchestrate such an ending
inviting his family, friends and neighbors,
fellow bards and kindred spirits, plus
acquaintances down through the ages

first, he re-wrote his will to settle
a few scores, and to send a few gifts
to worthy souls he hardly knew
but who did him a personal kindness
or showed a measure of tolerance
toward his most glaring foibles

next, he booked this grand hotel for a weekend
known for its ballroom and sumptuous banquets,
with charming rooms for the many travelers;
hired minstrels, mimes, and vaudevillians
along with the best dance bands in the land
to provide his guests with non-stop merriment

at the end of it all, he took center stage, himself,
said a few words, read a few poems,
and proceeded to *sing* the very last one
which had been set to music by friends,
surprising and delighting the crowd
with the way he did justice to the high notes

finally, he thanked them all for coming
and embraced them all in turn
then sent them on their way;

gave his family a few days to rest
before gathering them on Wednesday
whereupon he said his last fare-thee-wells

then drank the drink that put him to sleep
and his body was scattered out to sea
while his spirit took to the air

Ask No More Than in the Race

Pushing your boulder up the hill
tests your wherewithal and your will
slinking back down when it slips away
tests your faith in another day

dragging your cross through crowded streets
brings on that "high" of which no one speaks
the big surreal only you can see:
every lying face etched in your memory

ask no more than in the race
coming in last ain't no disgrace
when you get to show some maverick moves
while singing straight from your heartbreak shoes

good deeds done for who knows who
pays you back with a dream come true
as you drink your fill from the poet's gourd
and ride a ripple to the farthest shores

A roll of the dice
the scales of fortuity
-- I got no complaints